Dreaming Of
Dolphins

Claire Nicole Long

authorHOUSE®

AuthorHouse™
1663 Liberty Drive
Bloomington, IN 47403
www.authorhouse.com
Phone: 1-800-839-8640

Published by AuthorHouse   10/22/2012

ISBN: 978-1-4772-3937-7 (sc)
ISBN: 978-1-4772-3938-4 (e)

Chapter I

Seven year old Sophie awoke to hear her parents Anne and Richard talking softly down stairs. The sound of the hoover at the far end of the house and a cheerful humming by the busy housekeeper May kept her from falling back to sleep. Tossing her bedcovers to one side, Sophie made her way over to the window overlooking the pretty garden. Her eyes fixated on her favourite spot. The cobbled stone pathway that reached a pond under the old apple tree at the far end of the garden.

When Sophie was a toddler, it was here that she swore to everyone, fairies could be seen dancing around the pond, first thing in the morning. As she grew older, the fairies vanished and Sophie was no longer able to see or experience the magic. But to this day her visions and memories were still very strong.

Sophie dressed quickly and packed the last of her small, pink suitcase. She was sad to be leaving her family home and would miss her parents terribly, even if they were not always around. But it was only for a month or so and things would return to normal as soon as she was back. Today Sophie was travelling to Scotland to stay with Aunt Rosemary, who she had never met before. Her mother's sister was known to be eccentric and estranged from the family. Widowed and childless from an early age, she lived alone in the remote area of the Moray Firth situated beside the sea. Aunt

Rosemary was the only living relative left of Sophie's parents and had agreed to take in Sophie for the summer holidays.

Normally the Harrison family would be spending the summer holidays together flying out to their second home in Florida, America. It was such precious time when they could all be together once a year. But this year it wasn't to be. Anne and Richard were forced to sacrifice their holidays and continue working throughout the summer period, due to crises in both their busy career lives. As timing would have it the family's nanny Emily was called away to look after her seriously ill mother in Cornwall and did not know when she could return.

Anne and Richard had employed Emily from the Norlands nanny school in London, when Sophie was 6 months old. Anne was then able to return back to work. Emily lived as part of the family and was a godsend. She was 27 years old, single and totally devoted to Sophie. Sophie adored her but in Emily's heart she knew it was her parent's attention she craved the most. She too was sad to be leaving the Harrisons but knew that it was her mother who needed her desperately now.

Chapter 2

Richard and Anne

R ichard was a high flying businessman who owned an I.T consultancy company in Docklands London. He loved the buzz of the job and was happiest when he was pulling off major contracts with customers. Frequently he would travel out to America alone on business trips. The only down fall was seeing less of his family. He had to push the heartache aside of not seeing his wife and little girl knowing the benefits they would gain from his absence. The money bought rewards such as a luxury comfortable lifestyle and good education for Sophie. He hoped this was enough for now but could see the bitter disappointment on Sophie's face when he told her they wouldn't be together during the summer holidays . . . .

Richard had struck a deal with a new client involving huge amounts of money, which in turn would mean him managing the project from June onwards. The reputation of the company would expand through the roof bringing many opportunities along the way. No one was better qualified in this role than himself. If Richard didn't cease the challenge now in a flash it would be gone moving onto the next available company. Family life would have to be put on hold for a while . . . .

Sophie's mother Anne was an attractive woman with a flair for fashion and design. She too was career driven in running her own chain of fashion and boutique stores across London. Recently she had opened her third shop called Essentials in Kensington high Street. Anne was confident and determined to do well in all she put her mind too. She only wished she had more hours during the day to spend time with Sophie. But it was impossible with the new store opening and a staff shortage on her hands. She would have to run the new store for the summer as well as manage the business accounts for the two other shops. There would be no holiday this year. Her little girl was growing up so fast, but she tried to push the guilty feelings aside and hoped Sophie would one day understand. When Sophie was old enough she would one day work alongside her mother and eventually run the business. Anne had contacted her sister Rosemary as a last resort in the hope she would take care of Sophie for the summer. They were not the closest of sisters and spoke very little, but Anne felt she had no choice and was secretly surprised when Rosemary said yes. Maybe having a child around would be good for Rosemary in the light that she didn't have any of her own.

Chapter 3

Emily and Aunt Rosemary

After a particularly bad break up with her boyfriend at 18 years old. Emily had felt like she had been working in a dead end supermarket job that was going nowhere. So she decided to join the Norlands nanny school, which came highly recommended. Emily adored children and babies and wanted to make a career out of it. After she qualified her first family were the Harrisons. It was a good match. She clicked very well with the family, especially their daughter Sophie and so she had stayed for seven years now with the same family.

Emily loved the house and area and found her job extremely rewarding. Her only family was her mother who lived in Cornwall. She had been poorly on and off from high blood pressure and the devastating news had come early one evening that her mum had suffered a mini heart attack. She was recovering slowly but of course would need care and help at home for some time. Emily didn't waste another minute, telling her employers she must leave immediately and begin to pack her bags for Cornwall.

Aunt Rosemary had married very young at 17 years of age; she was very much in love with her husband. They were happily married for three years until tragedy struck and her husband was killed in a train crash. Aunt Rosemary was expecting a baby but the shock of her husband's death made her lose the baby.

As the years went on she became more and more reclusive and never married again, no one would replace her husband. She eventually moved out to a big old house in the Moray Firth to be beside the sea. Once retiring from being a school teacher, she was happy to be alone with her memories. Aunt Rosemary had lived like this for years and nothing had changed until Sophie had walked into her life . . . .

Chapter 4

Saying Goodbye

Downstairs Sophie's mother tidied whilst her father organised the luggage and car. Sophie was to fly to Scotland, boarding a plane alone for the very first time. After being dropped off at the airport by her father, she would then be escorted as a special minor through the airport and onto the plane. The stewardess in flight would take care of her and once landed the other side, Sophie would be met by Aunt Rosemary. The whole of experience of going alone was very daunting. It was scary enough to be going to a strange place to stay with an unknown relative. But there seemed no other choice and she tried desperately to be brave.

Anne turned to her daughter and hugged her tightly. "I will miss you darling and I love you very much" "you will have a wonderful time in Scotland and remember I am only a phone call away" daddy's waiting now" "I love you too mummy" Sophie whispered she tried hard to blink back the tears. She reached for her teddy and ran for the door. Saying goodbye was hard.

The rain was beating down on the windscreen and she clutched her teddy harder for comfort. The whole day seemed dark and depressing Sophie thought. Her father seemed engrossed in his own world, but suddenly sensing her nervousness, Richard put on some music. "Everything will be fine and you will have so much fun in Scotland you won't want to come home" "The holidays will fly by you'll see". As they drew into the airport the rain stopped and the sun shone brilliantly this cheered Sophie a little.

Holding hands they made their way with the trolley into departures. The queue was short and check in was quick. Sophie was introduced to her escort Sadie and her father kissed her goodbye. "I have to go now, be brave for daddy and I will see you real soon" then he was gone. Sadie took her hand and walked her quickly through passport control. The lady seemed nice enough and offered her some sweets. "They will stop your ears popping on the plane" So many noises and hundreds of people it was all so overwhelming. Next stop was the departure lounge. Wheelchair users, pushchairs and child minors were boarding first. So not much waiting around and before Sophie had time to think she was sitting comfortably on the air craft. The stewardesses kept coming up to see if she was ok and offered her a drink. Looking out of the window she felt a sudden excitement and kind of freedom that not many children her age would have experienced. In a way being an only child she was used to being by herself. The plane took off and Sophie dug out her Winnie the Pooh storybook. She felt content for now if not a little tired from the events of the morning.

Sleepily Sophie opened one eye as she felt the pressure of the plane gliding down. She must have drifted off whilst reading her story. The landing was a little bumpy but the stewardess assured her all was well. She sat and waited patiently whilst passengers got off first.

Chapter 5

The Arrival

Then it was Sophie's turn, guided by a stewardess off the plane and then handed over to another airport guide. They made their way to arrivals and onto passport control. Sophie suddenly spotted her pink suitcase going round the conveyer belt. After a quick trip to the toilet and a drink, she was heading through the airport towards a sea of faces where eagerly awaiting friends and families were looking out for their loved ones. Some people and taxi drivers had placards with names on so they could be recognised. Sophie didn't have the faintest clue what Aunt Rosemary looked like she had never seen a picture of her. But the airport guide took the lead and suddenly Aunt Rosemary was spotted with a big blue sign stating her name. She was a tall lady wearing a huge orange hat with purple flowers on it and a long yellow hippy dress. Not what Sophie had imagined at all. She also looked much younger. Aunt Rosemary was waving madly in her direction with a welcoming smile. Maybe this wasn't going to be so bad after all thought Sophie.

"Welcome to Scotland Sophie" She gave her a hug. "Well let's have a look at you, you are smaller than I imagined but the spitting image of your mother" Sophie smiled whilst Aunt Rosemary chatted on. "Come now I have a car waiting for us and I'm sure you are tired after your long journey" Sophie decided she liked Aunt Rosemary and they got to know each other a little on the thirty minute drive. Aunt Rosemary had her own personal chauffeur who escorted her everywhere, if ever she felt like driving herself there was a weekend car garaged at her house. The busy roads and towns disappeared whilst picturesque lakes and countryside replaced them. They drove over cattle grids and through small country lanes where the area grew more remote. Buildings vanished and there were no houses except for the odd cottage tucked away.

As they turned and approached a long gravely road Sophie caught glimpses of the sea and felt a familiar excitement building again.

Such a far cry from the busy hectic life style back in London. A huge Edwardian house loomed ahead of them surrounded by immaculately kept grounds. As they pulled up a barking noise came from the side of the house and a very playful black Labrador raced towards the car. "This is Jess, my three year old Labrador, hope you don't mind dogs, she's very friendly" Sophie was thrilled, she had never had a pet before and it looked like she now had a playmate for the summer. She stroked his velvety ears and he jumped up and licked her nose. "Down girl we don't want you getting too excited" Aunt Rosemary said. "Thank you driver lets go inside and I will show you around"

The five bedroom house seemed enormous but quite cosy despite its stark appearance outside." I have a housekeeper and a gardener who comes here once a week, occasionally my friend from the next village drops in, but they are the only visitors you will see". There are no annoying neighbours and we are we are quite out in the sticks you see, but that's the way I like it with nobody to bother me". Sophie relaxed for the first time and wondered what adventures laid ahead of her with so many lovely places to explore. This was going to be an interesting holiday she thought.

Chapter 6

Room With a View

"Let's go and find your room, it's all ready for you" Aunt Rosemary said. They slowly climbed the spiral stair case which seemed to go on forever. Sophie stared at the colourful backgrounds and figurines they looked like they were smiling down on Sophie with a magical knowing kind of look. The one that caught her eye the most was of a shimmering blue, silver dolphin leaping out of the sea. Sophie swore it had a twinkle in its eye.

Sophie's bedroom was down a long corridor towards the right wing of the house. As the door was opened light flooded the bedroom. "You have a sea view no doubt the seagulls will wake you in the morning." Aunt Rosemary smiled. "I will let you have some quiet time to unpack and adjust, then come down when you are ready. Tea will be waiting as I expect you are hungry after a long journey" The room was very spacious. There was a lovely wooden toy box with a woolly teddy bear on the front and an old rocking horse in the corner. It was filled with various toys that looked like they had never been played with, how strange Sophie thought as Aunt Rosemary didn't have children! Could she have bought all this just for me . . . .

The view was the most stunning with the rolling countryside and sea shore. To hear the waves lapping from Sophie's window was wonderful. Suddenly her thoughts returned to home as she remembered her little bedroom window overlooking her garden. She missed home, her parents and Emily and wondered what they were all doing now. Sophie felt the tears well up again. I must be grown up about it after all it was just a holiday and holidays must be enjoyed. With that thought she skipped down stairs to find Aunt Rosemary laying out an enormous tea. Jam sandwiches, scones, jelly and ice cream, cake she immediately felt ravenous and tucked in" I hope you like it Aunt Rosemary said" "I have rather a sweet tooth myself she chuckled to herself" "I do hope you will enjoy staying at the Moray Firth there is much to look forward to and explore here" "can't wait" Sophie said.

Aunt Rosemary observed she was a polite but quiet child. Understandable as it was a big change for her coming away without her parents for the first time. Aunt Rosemary already knew Sophie didn't see much of them and that must be hard for any child. So she was determined to see that Sophie would enjoy her stay here and there was so much freedom that came from living in the countryside that was perhaps different from her London home and surroundings. It would be good company for Aunt Rosemary and an opportunity to get to know her niece.

"Would you like to go and see the garden before bed" "yes please" Sophie was excited" At the same time Jess bounded up with a ball" "I think he wants to play too giggled Aunt Rosemary" Sophie and Jess played for an hour whilst Aunt Rosemary washed up and tidied the house. It was surprisingly nice to have a child running around and wondered what it would have been like if life had been different all those years ago. "Time to get ready for bed Sophie" she called through the kitchen window.

Laying in her pretty bed that night holding teddy, she began to drift off peacefully dreaming of the sea, dolphins and what exciting adventures would await her.

Chapter 7

A Brand New Day

A distant barking in Sophie's dream began to stir her from her sleep. Yawning and stretching she realised the noise was coming from the garden. She padded over to the window and was delighted by the sunny views of the countryside and sea. It was going to be a great day.

Quickly she dressed and headed downstairs. The smell of hot cross buns was lovely as she sat down for breakfast. "Did you sleep well dear" Aunt Rosemary asked "yes thank you my bed was very comfortable" After breakfast Sophie headed out doors and played ball with Jess in the magnificent gardens. Harry the gardener greeted Sophie; he was working hard in the grounds today.

Suddenly Jess disappeared through a gap in the tall hedge down the end of the gardens and Sophie chased after her following her barks. There appeared to be an overgrown path filled with wild flowers either side. The path sloped down further and further until she could hear the waves lapping on the shore. Then Sophie was there standing on a beautiful sandy beach with crystal clear water. This was a private beach, Aunt Rosemary's very own beach and Sophie had it all to herself. She had never known so much freedom; it was an incredible feeling unlike her protected, restricted up bringing at home. Aunt Rosemary's rules were to be home for lunch and to stay with Jess at all times.

Other than that she was free. The sun was hot tomorrow she must bring her swimming costume and bucket and spade.

As Sophie gazed out to the ocean something twitched and suddenly caught her eye, it was a glimpse of a dolphin's tail circling the shore. Sophie looked closer; the dolphin then somersaulted into the air as if performing tricks as the little girl watched on in awe. Then it vanished as quickly as it had arrived. The warm air and sea breeze had felt magical that morning. Sophie could hear Aunt Rosemary calling her from the house for lunch. As she ran back up the path, Sophie knew it wouldn't be long before she was back at the big blue sea once more!

Rain had set in for the next two days. Sophie watched the pitter-patter down the window pane and was desperate to head out again to the beach. To pass the time she played Ludo and Scrabble with Aunt Rosemary. They also had great games of hide and seek around the old house. Sophie enjoyed spending hours playing with the doll's house which had belonged to Aunt Rosemary as a little girl. Sophie liked to pretend the little figures were her mother, father and Emily her nanny. Aunt Rosemary even took her into the local village to buy her some nice summer clothes and more dolls house furniture to play with.

A letter arrived from mummy and daddy to say they would be visiting in two weeks, that seemed like a long way away but she was delighted that they would be coming to see her! Finally on day three the sun shone. Sunny and hot all day the weather forecast had said. "Sophie would you like to take a picnic lunch down to the beach?" Aunt Rosemary called "yes please" said Sophie and hurriedly went to pick up her bucket and spade. "Come on Jess" she said and kissed Aunt Rosemary good bye. The sea was the bluest, calmest sea she had ever seen, perfect for swimming. Sophie had always been a strong swimmer and taught from an early age.

After playing ball with Jess she settled on making a huge sandcastle, she was busy concentrating on putting a little flag on top of the highest steeple then it happened again.

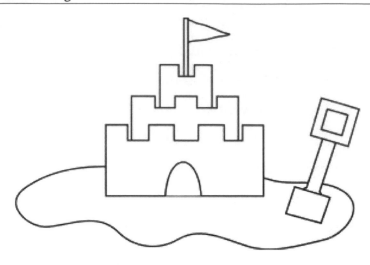

A silver darting movement out of the corner of her eye. It was the silver fin of the dolphin. It had returned again and seemed to be swimming closer this time, almost dancing with little jumps as if to invite her in. Curiosity got the better of her and already in her swimming costume, she waded in. Sophie didn't take her eyes off the dolphin in case he disappeared again. As she slowly approached it looked as if he were smiling at her. Quick as a flash he swam straight towards her and Sophie froze on the spot, what if he tried to attack her she was up to her waist in water. Dolphins were supposed to be friendly she thought. The dolphin circled her playfully and leapt into the air. She giggled and knew immediately she was safe. Carefully Sophie stretched out a hand and the dolphin nudged her gently with his nose. Extraordinarily Sophie began to hear a ringing kind of singing voice in her head that said" come and play with me". Sophie looked round, there was no one but her and the dolphin "is that you she whispered?"

"Yes it replied" she couldn't believe her luck a magical talking dolphin who wanted to be her friend. "What's your name?" "Starlight" it echoed back and like lightening Starlight was underneath her pulling her along as she gripped his fin. It was an amazing ride. He leapt in the air as she held on tight. The voice appeared in her head again "would you like to come and see my underwater home?" Hesitantly she replied "okay" "don't worry you will be safely returned" and looking into Starlight's eyes she knew it was safe to trust him.

In a split second, Sophie was under the water, finding she was able to breath, it was magical! Was this a dream, she pinched herself to find in was very real! Deeper and deeper what a strange sensation, but at the same time having so much fun. Golden lights whizzed past her and sea creatures of and sea creatures of all shapes and colours started to appear.

Could this be mermaids and water babies dancing on the sea bed? So pretty with curled golden locks, whispering their secrets. Beautiful coral gates entwined in tropical flowers. Still holding tightly to the dolphin's tail they sailed forward past colourful sea beds and sparkling sea shells. If there is a heaven then this is my dream of it Sophie sighed. She felt no fear only contentment to watch this beautiful picture unfolding before her eyes. Every time the dolphin looked at her she could hear his ringtone tone voice in her head. "Is this really happening to me" "yes because you are special" Starlight nodded. "It's like living in a fairy tale Sophie thought. "Come and meet my friends" Starlight pointed "Tinker, Winker, Serphine and Sunshine". "Wow" exclaimed Sophie "I thought mermaids were only girls. "No Tinker and

Winker are merboys. See Tinker winking at you". Then to her surprise they all took her hand and began dancing. It was an amazing and very liberating feeling all rolled into one. Next it was time for everyone to play a game of hide and seek behind rocks and reeds. Sophie couldn't remember the last time she laughed so much. Then Starlight nudged Sophie with his nose and sadly it was time to leave. Up they soared from the underwater world and resurfaced into the broad daylight. Together they rode all the way to the shore. "Will I see you again Sophie asked hopefully". Starlight gave her a twinkling look which and then was away like the speed of lightening. Sophie smiled and sat down next to Jess who was waiting patiently for her, watching the flick of his tail disappear into the sea. Would more adventures come her way she wondered? That night Sophie quickly fell asleep, dreaming of mermaids, fishes, music and wishes.

Chapter 8

Family Time

"Sophie your mummy and daddy are coming to visit today" Aunt Rosemary called. Over the coming days, with so much to think about, she had forgotten about being home sick. But now they were coming she couldn't wait to see them.

"I see the Moray Firth is working its magic on you" said Aunt Rosemary with a twinkling in her eye. "Enjoy and explore it's the best years of your life being a child" Sophie had a lovely day with her parents; she gave them a tour of the beach, the garden and told them all about her magical adventures under the sea. "Sophie does have a creative imagination" laughed mummy and daddy. "Yes" Aunt Rosemary said thoughtfully "she's a lovely girl". This holiday seems to suit her.

Anne noticed her rosy cheeks and how happy and healthy Sophie looked. This put her mind at rest the holiday was agreeing with Sophie. Aunt Rosemary and mummy were chatting away at lunch and Sophie was glad to see them getting on well and back in touch. Aunt Rosemary offered for them to stay the night but they would have to leave early next morning due to busy work schedules. "Another four weeks and you will be home" daddy said. Sophie was sad to see them go the next morning but she was enjoying her holiday and adventures so much she would actually be sad to leave Scotland now!

Aunt Rosemary and Sophie were becoming very close; they giggled, played games and swapped silly stories. Aunt Rosemary loved having a child around; it brought the house alive with fun and laughter which she had long forgotten herself as a child. Many happy memories of Aunt Rosemary's childhood with her and her sister Anne especially Christmas times were remembered again. Sophie loved to listen to these stories. I wish I had a little brother or sister Sophie thought to share the fun with. Sophie adored the attention she was getting as well as the freedom and space here. Aunt Rosemary as well as being her Aunt was like her best friend.

Chapter 9

A Close Call

The summer heat was beating down, So Sophie and Jess skipped eagerly down to the beach. "I wonder if I shall see Starlight today", she said to Jess woof she barked as if to encourage her. It had been a few days what with her parents visiting and shopping trips with Aunt Rosemary.

After playing on the beach nearly an hour and still no Starlight, she was feeling a little disappointed. Sophie decided to go for a swim to cool down. She was a good swimmer and dived under the water with her eyes open. Something blurry started to swim straight towards her. It must be Starlight but as her vision cleared the skin colour was much darker and whatever it was it had a twisted face that looked like it was smirking at her. It opened its mouth and all Sophie could see was yellow sharp teeth. Trembling she knew she was in grave danger and kicked her feet hard to swim to the surface. As she reached the top Jess was barking madly as if to warn her and started to wade in. A pointed fin now only ten yards away was circling her round and round and immediately she knew it was a shark.

Sophie closed her eyes, it was too late to get away, and she started to panic and splash her way back to the shore. Then from nowhere Starlight leapt into the air and crashed down into the ocean blocking the evil shark from her view. A wreathing, crunching sound as one fish hit against the other. The fight had begun. Sophie was still swimming and but not daring to look back and her limbs were beginning to ache. She must not give up whilst she still had a chance. Then all was calm and the waves had subsided where the dolphin and the shark had begun to fight. Next Starlight sped along and pushed himself under Sophie giving her ride back to shore. "Zinger" won't be bothering you anymore" Starlight reassured her. A shaking and shocked Sophie burst into tears "I never been so scared thank you for saving me" she cuddled into starlight in the shallow water. "Let me cheer you up I've been waiting to take you on a special adventure" his sparkling eyes and harmonious voice echoed. "I don't know is it safe"? Sophie whispered. "Perfectly" Starlight smiled, "okay" Sophie replied hesitantly. He circled Sophie and together they rode the tidal waves. "I have missed you" giggled Sophie. Next they soaring along the sandy sea bed under the water but Sophie never felt any pressure on her ears and could always talk without swallowing up the water. Through the golden gates they glided. There was music and clapping, singing and dancing surrounded by hundreds of mer people and children, fishes and dolphins.

"What's happening Sophie asked"? "You're invited to a special party, come and join my birthday celebration" said an excited Starlight. "Your birthday I didn't realise" "just happy to have you here" Starlight smiled. Winker the merboy came up winking at her and grasped her hand. Then everyone joined in and began dancing around in a circle singing happy birthday. "Watch this" Winker said and blew really hard in the water. Huge rainbow coloured bubbles floated up with Happy Birthday written on them. "You try Sophie" "Wow this is amazing, the best party I have ever been to!" A water baby named Angelica swam round putting underwater handmade flower necklaces on everyone. Some fishes nearby played harps and flutes the music was very euphoric. Starlight came up and guided her to a golden table which had golden chairs and golden cups. Floating above the table were disco balls reflecting all the colours under the water. The waters were sea horses pouring food and drink into various dishes. At the head of the table was what looked like a beautiful king and queen mermaid family? "They rule the underwater kingdom" said Starlight. "They are very kind people and always come to celebrate sea creatures birthday! They smiled and waved looking very curiously at Sophie. "I see we have a human child here, you must be the first we have ever had. Is your star sign a Pisces by any chance?" "Yes" breathed Sophie "Ah that explains it you are naturally a creature of the sea". A toast to Starlight "Happy Birthday and to welcome his very special friend Sophie". Everyone clapped.

As time flew on Starlight nudged her with his nose and Sophie knew it was time to go. She felt incredibly sleepy as she climbed on his back. The next thing Sophie remembered was slowly waking up on the beach with Jess barking at her. "Did I just dream that" she thought and then saw her costume and the little glimmering rainbow ribbon which had been tied to her finger, they were all wearing them at the party. She knew then it had once again been very real.

"Oh my goodness I must be very late, I must have been away hours" Jess chased after her as she raced back to the garden and up towards the house. Strangely her watch said exactly the same time as it had before she left to swim with Starlight. Maybe my watch has stopped she thought. Aunt Rosemary was in the kitchen, "hello my dear you have come back for an early tea, you must be very hungry" how strange Sophie thought, so time stands still while I'm in the magic underwater world. She would check this with Starlight next time she saw him.

Chapter 10

The Secret Room

The next day was raining and Sophie decided to explore the house some more, there was a room that had never been opened on the second floor and was always locked. I wonder why Aunt Rosemary never opens this. As she knelt down on the mat to spy through the key hole, something hard was underneath her knee. A very large rusty old key.

Maybe she shouldn't go in but curiosity got the better of her. Slowly turning the key she walked into a dark attic bedroom.

The curtains were pulled even though it was daylight. Sophie opened them and light flooded the beautiful room. There was a rocking chair, an old rocking horse, a toy box and a cot with a new teddy in. The cot bed was made up but looked like it had never been slept

It must have been a nursery she gasped but Aunt Rosemary doesn't have any babies or children, how odd. Sophie explored the toy box and found some dolls and soldiers to play with. Next she rode the large rocking horse which was perfect for her height.

As she rocked back and forth something captured the corner of her eye. On the dressing table in the middle was a blue and white snow globe. Sophie wondered over to pick it up, I must be careful not to break it. The globe looked very old and inside was a sparkling dolphin with pretty fishes and mermaids dancing all around. She turned it over to watch the bubbles and snow whizz around. It looks awfully like Starlight she thought. Suddenly the dolphin inside winked at her and began moving with the fishes and mermaids dancing around him. Delighted Sophie watched on, this definitely was a magic house even the paintings would wink at you if they caught you off guard. And everywhere that Sophie went the magic seemed to follow.

A creaking in the corridor broke her concentration and she quickly put the globe down. It went still. Aunt Rosemary had appeared in the door way not looking too happy! Then her expression turned to sadness and tears were rolling down her face. "Oh dear I really have been very naughty Sophie thought. "I can't blame you for being curious" Aunt Rosemary said. "It's been a long time since this room has been opened" She sat down on the bed and patted it for Sophie to come and sit beside her. She told Sophie everything from when she was married and how she lost her husband in the tragic accident and then her baby over the shock. "So you see I have lived like this for years" and Sophie now understood the reasons for her sadness. Sophie reached for her hand, "I'm so sorry and I'm sorry I opened the room" whispered Sophie. "Not at all, it needed to be opened and I think it now has a new purpose we can turn it into a playroom for you". Aunt Rosemary hugged Sophie and told her to bring the other toys and dolls house in. The cot was taken out and they both spent the whole afternoon rearranging the room. This seemed to help Aunt Rosemary a little, although the sadness would always remain. Sophie then remembered the snow globe and asked Aunt Rosemary about it. "Yes that was mine when I was a little girl" Aunt Rosemary said with a familiar twinkling in her eye. "It will bring you many happy dreams and good luck, you may keep it." Thank you Sophie said gratefully. "I think I already know the Dolphins name" said Sophie, "so do I" said Aunt Rosemary smiling knowingly, "now that's another story . . . ." "Have a look underneath the globe" she said as she walked out of the playroom leaving Sophie to play. Sophie picked it up and turned it over and engraved on the bottom was the name *Starlight*.

Chapter II

Sophie's Last Adventure

The holidays had flown by so quickly at Aunt Rosemary's and tomorrow Sophie was to return home. It was good news to hear that her parents would be home for the next two weeks on an overdue holiday. Emily the nanny would be returning after this holiday period, her mother had recovered well. Sophie was looking forward to seeing them all again, but would miss the Moray Firth with Starlight and all its magic along with Aunt Rosemary and her funny old house. Aunt Rosemary had said she could return for more holidays soon and definitely back for next summer.

One last day to spend with Starlight and she couldn't wait to see him. Hopefully he would be there. She could hardly contain her excitement as she raced down to the sea and this time Starlight was already waiting for her very close to the shoreline. Sophie dived in and together they were playfully spinning around and swimming underwater. Starlight already knew this was Sophie's last day and had organised a party as a fond farewell. In this land it seemed there were forever parties which was fantastic. As they slipped down deep into the oceans more and more dolphins and fishes swam alongside them. Golden starts were trailing and floating everywhere. They all know you are leaving today and they want to make it special for you. Sophie felt an overwhelming happiness. At the tropical gates there was a treasure chest spilling with gold and silver it had Sophie's name on it. A leaving present from us sang starlight. Wow thank you exclaimed Sophie.

Starlight and Sophie sat down at the table with all their friends and the fish began to serenade them. Lots of delicious food was served by penguin waiters. A dolphin cake was presented to Sophie with her name on. Next came a show with mermaids and merboys on a silver stage in front of all the tables. They were floating and performing somersaults which reminded Sophie of a circus show she had been to see in London. The King and Queen had then arrived to join in the celebrations. Come and join us they echoed in a melody voice towards Sophie. Holding hands with the King, Queen and Starlight together they all swam onto the stage for what seemed like hours of dancing fun. All too soon Starlight signalled to her and it was time to leave. "Come and see us on your next holiday shouted Tinker and Winker. One of the water babies ran up and hugged her so tight, Sophie kissed her good bye. If it wasn't for her my friends and family at home I should like to stay forever thought Sophie. As they reached the shoreline, Sophie cuddled Starlight for the last time "when I come back on holiday you will still be here won't you. "Always" said Starlight with that familiar twinkle in his eye and he handed her a white sea shell necklace to remind her of so many wonderful adventures she had that would come her way. It had shining pearls on it. Goodbye Starlight" I will miss you and thank you for everything" You are welcome and come back soon". With a beaming smile and a flick of his tail he was gone. Sophie felt like crying, but knew it wasn't the end and the tears were happy tears for everything she had experienced under that magical sea. Her thoughts were interrupted by Jess barking on the beach. The holidays were ending tomorrow and soon she would be home, but Sophie would never forget these amazing adventures as she skipped down towards the path wearing her pretty sea shell necklace.

"Have you packed all your things dear?" called Aunt Rosemary up the stairs. "Yes, nearly ready". One last look around her pretty room. Sophie had so much fun in the house also and couldn't wait to return.

Mummy and daddy were already waiting downstairs ready to pick her up. Their holiday had already started and they decided to drive up to Scotland to collect her. The two sisters seemed much closer and were going to keep in touch. Aunt Rosemary had already invited the Harrison family up for the Christmas holidays; she had decided she had spent too many Christmases on her own. Anne and Richard were delighted and so it was all arranged. Sophie didn't have to wait long and now she could already look forward to her next holiday.

Richard had successfully pulled of his major contract so would definitely be taking more time off work in the future and Anne had hired an employee to do the admin and accounts leaving her more time to spend with Sophie after school and at weekends. Everything is falling into place Sophie thought as she looked back waving goodbye at Aunt Rosemary who then returned the gesture with a wink and a smile just like Starlight and Winker do always do . . . . Hand in hand the Harrison family walked down the front garden path happy to be together again.

THE END

Lightning Source UK Ltd.
Milton Keynes UK
UKOW050251061112

201724UK00007B/5/P